Timeless Sisters

A Novella About Love in All of Its Dimensions

John Schmidt

Path Publishing

Amarillo, Texas

Path Publishing
4302 SW 51st #121
Amarillo, Texas 79109-6159
USA
Path@PathPublishing.com
www.PathPublishing.com

Cover by Path Publishing and CreateSpace, with illustration by Joni Beckner.

This volume is also a Smashwords ebook, which can be ordered on many apps or at Smashwords.com.

Story originally published in *Heroes, Angels and Miracles* by the same author.

To order copies, see Books and Ebooks by John Schmidt in the About the Author and the Publisher section at the end of the book.

ISBN-13: 978-1-891774-72-0
ISBN-10: 1-891774-72-7

Printed in the United States of America

CONTENTS

DEDICATION

I dedicate this book to all of the children in the world who grow up without one or both parents.

ACKNOWLEDGMENTS

To W.W., the story editor who helped with this story and several in *Heroes, Angels and Miracles*, where it was originally published.

To the many writers over the years I have read, especially Charles Dickens, who taught me much about fiction writing.

Chapter 1

In a solar system not far from ours was once a world much like Earth. They called their world Timeless, for they realized they were Spirit beings. Unfortunately, they could not break the hold fear and war had on them. This is the story of how love was allowed to change a part of Timeless to peace, which eventually spread to their whole world and created a world of peace. It is a timeless story, for any world that wants to hear.

On the small but significant planet of Timeless was the kingdom ruled by King Tor, who was a fairly wise and thoughtful ruler, never the man to start a war or finish one. If another country wanted to fight his people for their land, he would send delegates, musicians, and carts of delicious food and fine wine, which would be especially strong for the occasion. He would then wait for them to either request more food and wine or find someone else to fight. So adept was he at his diplomacy of merriment that his people escaped war for an entire generation, something no one ever remembered happening before. And they were all glad to stay out of war.

King Tor was blessed with two daughters, or should I say, blessed with one and learned patience by the other. The king's wife, Terese, had died years before, in childbirth or some secret calamity, and left him to raise two daughters. The oldest was fair, with blond hair, Philintine her name. A beauty all admired, but so cold a heart had she, so merciless could she be, that no man would want her for wife, no more than he would live for the love of a snake.

The second daughter, Anesia, was puny and frail, suffering a limp caused by falling from a horse when she was eight. But she could be mistaken for her sister from the back, if in their mother's old, stately, padded robe with its high collar at back and her hair hidden under a crown, which the two of them wore once as children in a game of pretend. Her limp could be noticed, but seldom was, except by her. She thought herself secretly ridiculed by the court. She was not, for in her heart was a deep love for all, including the animals about the castle. Everybody seemed to love Anesia, though she could do nothing of note—not even ride a horse.

Philintine was jealous of Anesia—very jealous. If her younger sister died or was married off to a neighboring kingdom, she would care not at all. Philintine's cold heart ruled her life, or so it seemed.

The sisters lived with their father in a beautiful castle, long and wide, with turrets on each corner and two by the great gate. Behind the castle could be seen hills that made the whole scene picturesque. Not everyone in the kingdom lived in the castle, of course. Most had their homes, sheds, livestock, and manufacturing buildings on the farms and lands around the castle. Each day, many of the inhabitants, some from far out, made their way into the castle. They came either through the main gate or the second gate on the back side, through which the main road in the kingdom continued. In at sunup and out again at sundown, they entered to work in the shops, traded for supplies, paid their taxes, or in an emergency sought protection from an attack by foreigners, which never came because of King Tor's brave knights and his policy of free food and wine for all foreigners.

Chapter 2

But as rumor would have it, such an attack was coming from a small army sent by a neighboring land. If there was no army to be found, all the better. Tor and his men would spend a few days ravaging parts of the land for legions of boar and bring back meat for dozens of people—and thus, he would be the hero of all. As King Tor gathered most of his knights in the courtyard, he waved to Anesia, standing behind a second story window. She blew kisses to him.

Once all were ready to go, Tor leaned down to his oldest daughter. "On previous excursions, I have left Matti in charge. However, my dear, I think you are old enough to practice queen for a few days. Someday I shall not come back from one of these excursions and you or your sister will be queen."

Shall be me, thought Philintine.

"I have told Matti and the court of my decision. Farewell, my love." He held out one of his strong hands, which rumor had it, were strong enough to grab a small sow by the throat and suffocate it.

She took his hand, somewhat reluctantly.

"Be good to your sister. Be good to us all." Letting go her hand, he turned his horse and headed for the west gate.

Philintine looked up at her smiling sister. *Such a fool you are, to hold so dear the man who killed our mother.*

As Tor left the castle, Philintine thought, *At last I am queen. It is time I put this country into safe hands.*

Chapter 3

That evening, into the throne room came Darien, the king of the country that bordered Tor's kingdom on the north. All countries were small, and they made alliances with each other in times of war. Always welcome in Tor's kingdom, Darien loved Anesia, and Philintine knew that all too well. Darien said, "I have come to see your father about a matter of great importance."

Philintine looked to those behind him. "Darien, please dismiss your escort so we may speak privately. You will be safe with me. I have dismissed my people. You will speak to Father in a while."

Darien was suspicious. He knew everyone called her The Snake, for her coldness and her calculating mind. But he consented, asking his guards to wait outside. Once the throne room doors were closed and they were alone, Philintine sat on the throne. Darien thought it odd, but said nothing.

"One day I shall be queen of our bountiful land with its grapes as far as one can see in all directions. Would you like to own this property?"

"I would rather possess another." His love for Anesia filled him quietly.

"Your land is beautiful, and next to the sea. We are landlocked and small."

"The sea unfortunately makes for unwelcomed visitors."

"Invaders?"

"We do well enough, and we will protect you. They have to cross our grains before reaching your grapes."

"But what from the other three directions? Would you save us then?"

"Friendly countries surround you. If one of them were in danger, we would hear of it and come to Anesia's—I mean, your aid."

"You would do this to save my sister?"

"I would do anything for your sister."

"Even lose your army in defending her?"

"Would not be lost. But defending her would be my life."

Philintine remembered the three of them as children, Darien coming twice a year with his father, the two kings hunting boar while they and children of the court played together. Years later, Darien came as a young teen and his interests in Anesia became serious. When Darien's father was killed three years before in a battle, defeating an invasion force from a nation far off, Darien had become the young king—one worthy of the title, for his people admired him for his courage and fairness.

"You have come for my sister's hand?"

"I wish to speak to your father."

"No thank you." He noted that when she earlier said he would be able to talk to her father she had been lying. "When did he leave?"

"This morning."

"In which direction? Perhaps I can find him."

"No one can find Father. Once no army is discovered, he enters himself into the deepest woods, where boar is best, and is lost until the wine runs out—or the boar—whichever comes first."

"May I speak to Matti, please?"

"Matti?"

"The wisest and most beloved counselor of all our lands."

"I know who he is, though I doubt your praises are warranted. On this occasion, Father made me queen before leaving. I wear this robe that was my mother's."

Darien sighed. *A grave mistake by him—must have been exceedingly drunk at the time.*

"Can I help you?" She came close to him, goblet in hand. "They say you are looking for a wife, to align your kingdom with a stronger power."

"I need no wife for that. We are strong enough."

"We are weak from wine. We need you."

"Your wine sends opposition in all directions, falling off their horses in gaiety. You do not need me to save you. Your father has done well."

She turned from him angrily, "Father, Father. All sing praises of an old drunk who kill—let my mother die."

"I'm sorry your mother did not live to see her fine daughters."

"Daugh-*ter*. One a dove, one a snake. Or have you not heard the common opinion of me?"

"I did not come here to discuss rumor or opinions. If your father is not here and Matti is disposed, then I shall return home."

"Don't go. Stay the night. No reason to sleep twice along the road when you can have comfortable beds. You can see Matti in the morning, if you insist. But don't go." She put down the goblet and came close again. "When we were children, you once found me fair of form and face." "I thought you a good friend."

"Why my sister and not me?"

"The gardener cannot always tell which flower is to be picked. Perhaps God, Who makes all flowers, moves His hand to choose one."

"Be sensible. Our kingdoms are next to each other." She touched his shoulder. "I need a friend."

"May I say, Philintine, rumor has it that you were once in love with the noblest knight in your land, Noron. Why, then, would you wish my hand rather than the one you love?"

Love is so silly, she thought, but said, "Do you realize the power our two kingdoms would have once united?"

"Mine is strong enough. Stronger still is your father's wine that protects your castle better than the moat around mine. I wish to be told where my room is."

She removed her hand. "You would marry Anesia in an instant if she were queen."

"I would marry her if she were the least maid in the land."

Philintine smiled. "A king, to look upon a maid? I doubt that."

"My heart says so."

"I do not trust hearts. I believe in calculated reason, like a strong tree builds roots in familiar ground."

"But the heart is like a bird that flies over trees for a greater view."

"And is eaten by the hunter's hawk."

"I will not argue metaphors with you."

"But you will not listen to reason."

"In my country, the laws are reasonable enough. But without a heart to balance them, they are but cold script on parchments. No blood flows in them."

"My people's blood may flow if not defended mightily enough."

"Your father defends you well, in his own way."

"My father is a fool. He chases boar, not men."

"Boars have sharp horns, but not swords as men, and present no threat to your sovereignty."

"So you agree with his foolishness?"

"I wish I had it, or some of it. As water in a stream looks weak, it does in time break rocks. So I say, wine has greater strength than walls. With his wine and high walls, I doubt anyone will bother you for yet another generation."

"Then you, too, are a fool."

"You call 'fool' a man who you moments ago suggested marriage to?"

"I have a dream: to insulate this kingdom from all invaders. For that, I will need your help, and those of the other kingdoms around us."

"Greater alliances between our kingdoms have also been discussed at my court, though the legions you fear are mostly in your mind. Your kingdom is secure."

"Not enough." She carefully chose her words. "We could, you and I, transform the region into our own and be so strong that no one would attack us. Kingdom by kingdom we would make alliances into a body of one."

"You speak of it like piling rocks into a mountain. Why can you not let the terrain lie as it is? These invaders you fear are far away. My father, by his death and the deaths of many valiant soldiers and knights, discouraged kingdoms so far away that some of them you have probably never heard of. But by making our region a fortress through alliances, you bring other regions closer. Think on this, I pray you. We are now small kingdoms, but if our region is made one, kingdoms in regions about ours will, seeing our united strength, be forced to unite. In time, fearing our restlessness, they might swiftly attack us first."

"My plan is totally defensive."

"How do they know that? And if you should die, the next Alliance Commander of our six or ten kingdoms may be a warring sort and get twenty kingdoms to blood when none should have been. By your singular fear, you could in time not only bloody those nearest you, but other regions. How many thousands would first die to attain our alliance if some interior kingdom wanted not to join us and was forced to—and later, how many tens of thousands in regional wars? You would surely die in this very room by assassin's knife."

She drank the rest of her goblet of wine and poured more.

He looked closely at her hair. "Why does a woman of such beauty, hair of golden rays of sun, put blackest night in her imagination and let it boil? Why should she want her father's red wine turned to blood? It is said your father was a mighty soldier as a young man, but after his third or fourth battle did enter this room and speak to your counselor, saying the blood he shed could never be washed from his hands till the day he died. He took to full drink that day, and somewhat ironically, has kept himself and all his people battle-free since."

More to herself she said, "I heard it was a time soon after my mother's death." Then back to Darien, "But someday, war again, perhaps."

"Let God above postpone that day to some far-off time and enjoy your days of wine and roses. The wine be your father, and the rose, your sister."

"So you will not have me as queen?" She sat on the throne.

"I did not say that. I do believe in Heavenly Purpose beyond the highest queen or king that keeps the peace, even if it be, for some lands, through wine. Some in my court would have me marry you for the same reasons you have outlined, but I have refused their ideas. Better to marry for love than spend one night in a State-arranged bed."

"My mother was arranged. Perhaps why Father let her go so easily."

"I do not know how long I shall live. But I would rather have a short reign of love than a long one of inner sadness. I will defend you, and your sister. Even if she be in my kingdom, I will defend you."

"There—" She tore into his words like hawk into a sparrow's flesh. "You have come to ask for my sister's hand. Thus your eagerness to see Father." She came toward him.

"What if I have? Is there any harm in love?"

"When unguarded by firmness of mind, the State is in great danger. She would be too weak a queen for you. You need someone strong, like me."

"Normally I am head-guided, but will, now, say what I feel: I feel you are led most by fear and passion, but cover it over with the robe of State."

"You doubt my sincerity?"

"I say what I feel at this moment."

"So do I! Your room is on the north end of the main hall, next to the window above the pond for watering horses. A room for your men is next door. If you wish, you have my permission to jump from the window into the pond if you need a bath."

He laughed. "I, or my couriers, have never received so childish diplomacy in any court we have ever visited. Though, I will not tell your father your words, but pass quietly into the halls and to my evening's stay." He bowed at the head and left the room, respectfully closing the door behind him.

Chapter 4

Darien hardly slept the whole night. Though the bed was soft, one of the softest he had ever lain on, his soul was greatly concerned. The woman he loved more than any other might never be his—if a jealous, wicked sister ever became queen. How could this happen in a world as advanced as his own?

Finally, he fell asleep, but awoke early. He dressed and left his room. He did not awaken his men in their room, preferring to find the kitchen he remembered in his childhood, where biscuits and meat enough were available even this early in the day. He wanted to be alone.

Turning a corner, he noticed Anesia for an instant, passing across another corridor that led outside. He knew she liked to roam in the fields and befriend small animals. Should he pursue her? He might never see her again if Philintine had her way. He ran after her. "Anesia."

"Darien?" She turned to the face she loved most to see. "When did you arrive?"

"Last evening. Your sister banished me to my room. Is she really queen? She acts as if she were queen already."

"Temporary queen. Father will restore order upon his arrival."

"I would like to speak to Matti. Where is he?"

"Usually in his room or in the study. But how can he help you?"

"I have come to ask for your hand."

"*My* hand?"

"Why do you seem so surprised?"

"We heard you were seeking a queen of some powerful land to better guard your borders."

"My father died guarding borders. And my uncle before him. And my grandfather. Which led me to ponder, why should I not follow in your father's footsteps, years free of war where wine is shared?"

"I am honored that you would have me, a cripple."

"Your limp is hardly noticeable. You think all the stars in the sky shudder at your limp, when their spirits but dance in happiness for your viewing them. No one at your court notices, I assure you. And never me."

She took his extended hand. "Then if your love be true, ask Father. Consult with Matti if need be."

"I ask of Matti that he watch over you till your father returns."

"He will, and God will. Matti will be most glad for the news of your proposal. But tell not my sister. Her rage—"

"I may already have."

"—is unpredictable." She squeezed his hand. "When we were children—"

"I vowed to love you."

"A girl cannot depend on a boy's vow. But must wait for the man to appear."

"A man, now."

"And a king. I feel so blessed."

Darien saw Philintine in the distance behind Anesia. "Your sister patrols the halls. I to the kitchen, then to Matti before home. I will not anger her further." He kissed Anesia's hand and disappeared around a corner.

Anesia waited for her sister to come closer.

"I saw him with you."

"We were not hiding."

"He will most surely marry *me*."

Anesia said, disbelieving, "I think not. He—" She held her tongue.

"What? What do you know that you cannot tell me?"

"Nothing."

"Do you fear me?"

"You have certain powers as temporary queen—"

"Queen."

"'Temporary queen,' Matti calls it."

"Matti is a fool, as are you. Do you not understand that matters of State must take precedence over our little wills. Our country needs to marry Darien's army for our own protection."

"Matti said—"

"Do not quote Matti to me."

"Then father said—"

"Nor Father. Do not quote *men* to me, Anesia. Men killed your mother. Do you understand? Men killed Darien's father." She held her sister's head in her hands and kissed her forehead. "Do you not see I wish only to protect you—us?"

"I do not know what to think." Her eyes looked down.

"Because you are thinking by the heart. Use your brain for thinking, Anesia, and see clearly what is needed between *us*, and between two countries."

"I will try."

Philintine released her sister and stepped away. "You are a lover of animals, are you not?"

"Yes."

"And you have gotten over your fear of horses."

"Not really. I still possess the limp that one of them gave me."

"But you could learn to ride again."

"I fear for my other foot—or my life."

"I ride all the time."

"But you are—" she stopped.

"What?"

"So much like a man."

"I have always tried to be the son that Father wanted. If I could cut off these breasts and grow muscles in arms great enough to crack open a man's skull with an ax, I would. As I am, I can but think as a man, and thus compensate Father for what I am not."

"Perhaps he does love you for what you are."

"He does not. He loves you. When you were a girl he would comb your hair for the longest time and you two would talk of animals and harvests."

She came back toward her sister. "He would leave my hair for the handmaiden's strokes." She turned away again. "If Darien wants your hand, and you wish his, who better to tell Father than you?"

"Is that my place?"

"Tomorrow morning you can ride after Father and tell him yourself."

"In a wagon, I pray."

"A horse, a fine horse, my finest—"

"Not your gray stallion—"

"A mare, a mare. I do know something about animals, Anesia, at least horses."

Anesia smiled in disbelief. "Dear sister, I am afraid of horses."

"Release your fears."

"I don't know how to ride."

"We can teach you this afternoon."

"Half a day to learn?"

"Strap you on, if we must. You won't fall off and you won't die."

"Dear—"

"No…protests. I have made my second official decision of my administration. Darien going home and you finding Father. I'll point you in the right direction, send Noron and another knight with you. Noron knows all of Father's favorite places. The three of you can find him. My riding clothes will fit you. Clear enough? Now, no protests. Be gone." And Philintine was gone, around a corner.

Anesia was left standing alone, shocked and afraid.

Chapter 5

Philintine was sitting in her day chamber when a knock came to the door. "Come in."

Anesia entered and closed the door behind her.

Philintine noticed she looked tired, even anxious, but said nothing.

"I had my lesson."

"Good. You will find Father in no time."

"Father could be anywhere."

"The stars will guide you."

"How can you do this to me?"

"Darien, you love?"

"Yes."

"Then go tell Father of his proposal."

"There has been no proposal."

"Intended proposal. And live happily ever after with the man of your dreams."

"I do not dream of him."

"All women dream of some man. Even me."

"And who is your man?"

"You have won him. Delight in your victory, which you gained by sitting and clapping, as you won him when you were a girl and he first visited us. I knew then, but stubbornly held on to the possibility of him loving me. Until yesterday. You have won the contest. So be content." She rose and looked out the window at the courtyard below.

"My horse is not content."

"The most gentle mare I possess. I didn't give you my stallion."
She smiled at the thought of doing just that. "Him, only I can
handle."

"If you love Darien and me, why send me off on a ride where I
might fall and become a double cripple?"

"He would love you if you were confined to a chair the rest of your
life."

"Can't we wait for Father to return?" She joined her sister at the
window.

"I am queen. That is my command."

"Temporary queen."

"*Queen*. We have been through this before and it changed nothing."

Anesia paused, then said, "Why do you hate me?"

"I do not hate you."

"Then why do you hate our beloved father? Or do you hate me for
loving Father?"

"If you are fond of a drunken king, that is your problem. If by your
defense of him whom I hate—there, I said it openly now—if my
hate spills over to you, overlook my actions. I will not hurt you.
But do not tempt me by disobedience."

"They say that pouring vinegar into new wine will spoil it. So, too, can hate spoil a nation?"

"More harm than what *he* has already done to it?"

"A generation of peace cannot be all bad."

"Begun soon after our mother's death."

"Do you still believe in the old tale that he killed her? You know she died in childbirth."

"*His* story."

"The midwife claimed—"

"Whom he sent packing." She turned, very close to Anesia's face. "Do you believe, in your infantile mind, that he who sent the midwife packing—banished from the kingdom—and silenced the words of the doctor and the handmaids at the threat of death— that his story is true?"

"If it is true he killed her—"

"If?"

"It is true, I guess… Dear sister, if Father did accidentally kill her, I have forgiven him."

"Which I cannot do." She looked again out the window.

"I refused long ago, the rumors, which you now may confirm. Yet my forgiveness has not sealed my heart, while your unforgiveness has turned you—"

"Into a snake?"

"No. Into a hard woman who can still forgive. Who has a heart."

"Does a snake have a heart?"

"It must, for it moves."

They paused, each looking out the window in silence.

Philintine was first to speak. "For all your disbelief in my actions, I do so love our land. And would sacrifice my happiness for its defense. Do you believe that?"

Anesia said a quiet, "Yes."

"I am no fool. The snake that tempted the first woman may tempt me to act too forcefully, and Father may send me to my room for my 'temporary' actions, but I feel confident that I can convince him that what I have done is for the best."

"I still must ride in the morning?"

"That is best."

Anesia walked to the door. She turned back to her sister, the light falling on her from heaven. "Whatever you do to me, I will always love you." Anesia left the room.

Chapter 6

About an hour later, Philintine was sitting on the throne, deep in thought, eyes closed, almost half asleep. She had been drinking her father's vintage brew.

Her thoughts were interrupted by someone saying, "We have matters to discuss."

She opened her eyes and found the face. It was Matti.

"We need to discuss this *ride* you have planned for your little sister."

"Do we?"

"Yes, dear Philintine."

"Queen."

"Queen?"

"You doubt my authority?"

"You have no authority—except that gained in a few passing words by your father."

"He said he had spoken to you and the court."

"I was instructed to allow you to make small decisions, of no great importance—"

She rose and stood, elevated above him. "I have his authority."

"Nothing that would endanger the State—or your sister."

"I have authority." She moved away.

"Under the law, you are queen only if he should die. And that is very unlikely. There has been no ritualized passing, no abdication of power by him to you. Do you understand, my dear?" He followed behind her.

She turned. "I have authority!"

"You have responsibility. And your actions thus far have stated plainly that you are not ready to be queen, not of this country or any country. You have done more to harm our relationship with Darien in one day than any person or any single act in the recent history of our countries. Our diplomacy has been carefully crafted by me and others for a generation, and it will not be undermined by a girl who drinks herself into thinking she is queen!"

She moved away again.

"This attempt 'to find Father' that you have planned for your sister—do you jest?"

"It's just a ride."

"On a horse she has ridden once—and she has told you she still fears horses—over unfamiliar roads, through woods to some unforeseen destination probably miles from your father—"

"Noron will be with her, and a knight of his choice."

"I know Noron, have for his six years here—"

"Seven."

"He will take care of her, and that is some relief. But when your father returns, I pity you when he finds out that you sent her after him. What his anger may do, I do not know."

"He may kill me?"

"No, but—"

"As he did my mother—"

Matti paused briefly. "Your mother died at Anesia's birth time."

"They say…"

"I was there."

"In the room? You saw her die as the baby was taken from her body?"

"Well, no, but—"

"Do not bother me with 'but's'." She walked to her goblet of wine, drank the rest of it, and poured another.

"Please do not drink so much wine. We have powerful points to discuss here."

"I can think better with it."

"Given your decisions in but a day-and-a-half, I think you should abstain for the rest of your life."

She sipped more wine.

"They say you once had an affinity for Noron."

"Had."

"He taught you to ride, and you liked him?"

"He is a good man. I may have liked him."

"It could be that he should be your husband one day."

"There is no Point of Law against a queen taking a knight as a husband?"

"You are not yet queen—"

"I am. Soon. I feel it."

"No law against it. But leave Darien to his plan with Anesia. Was a match made in Heaven."

"I do not believe in Heaven."

"Your mother did, whose robe you now wear."

"She is there, then, and I am here."

"I beg you, let Anesia stay off the horse."

"*You*—beg?"

"I ask. I implore."

"She rides tomorrow."

Matti paused—then said slowly, but with increasing vigor. "I will hold you personally responsible for any injury to her. And if she be injured, I will counsel your father that you not be queen before your sister, but only after. Do you understand me?"

"I hear your words."

"I have been his counselor since before your mother, and Tor will listen to me, especially when Darien and Anesia tell their stories."

"Do not jest with me, Matti. Only a fool, jests. Would you play the fool or be Counselor?"

"I would be Counselor to a girl too much with wine who thinks she is queen, but only hears sounds."

She sat again on the throne, placed the goblet to one side, and stared straight ahead. "You hate me, too."

"I do not. Never."

"I wish only what is best for this country."

"As do I. And sacrificing your sister makes no sense."

"Don't you think I have dreamed of this time, when I would be queen and we would defend our country rightly, not by wine diplomacy?"

"We are a tiny nation, almost the smallest anywhere. Do you really believe we could raise an army that would frighten others away?"

"We could with Darien."

"But do we need to?" He kneeled beside her. "Do listen to an old man. Pretend I am not Counselor to you, but friend—who had every male member of his family lost in some battle or another. Who was only excused because of his smallness of form, too weak to hold a sword, much less carry one to battle."

"Could have been an archer."

"But found a talent in books. And, though odd it may seem to you, a nation goes by its history. One who knows history and the law can be more valuable over time than any one soldier or archer. Thus I was set aside, perhaps like the best wine for an occasion of State."

He looked down for a moment. "I am not greatly gifted. But I have been sent out time and again to negotiate tender affairs of State or convince a rival king to not shed the lives of thousands of men, on both sides, in order to gain a vineyard that will pay him free wine forever at no expense. And I feel, in my way, I have saved the lives of thousands. You would not be sitting here without our wine diplomacy. Your sister would be married far off to a man she does not love."

"As was my mother."

"Yes, perhaps. I do not delve too closely into the hearts and loves of others, so to not intrude."

"A *bought* queen, received to gain the favor of a stronger power. A royal deal."

"It happens everywhere. But, you see, between Darien and Anesia is a double gift. Not only do two States align, but two lovers. Do you not see the wisdom in this? Let them alone. Take Noron, and let Darien be wed to *us*. You have all to gain and nothing to lose. But if she be injured on the horse, you may lose that fated union."

She continued to look straight ahead. "You are shrewd, Matti. Shrewd. Were I so cunning…"

"You are. You are bright of mind. I loved to teach you law; you took to it quickly. I can recall you as a girl sitting on a log in the country, the sun in your long, golden hair. I delighted in you then. I do still." He put his hand on her arm. "Love is not passed over by

31

time."

"I believe you. Somehow, though wine tempt me to blackness, I believe you. But Anesia rides tomorrow. She rides to Father."

"I have grown too old to be Counselor." He removed his hand. "I cannot persuade the golden-haired girl to not place in danger the one who clapped loudest for her running and somersaults. They say a snake, one day in the woods, ate your heart. I never believed them. Until today. Perhaps one did..." He stood up and walked slowly toward the main door.

"It's just a ride."

Without looking back, "I will hold you responsible under God and the kingdom. I pray you change your mind before the morning." At the door, he looked back briefly—not to judge, but to quietly observe the girl he once knew—who had, along the way, failed to become the woman he dreamed she would be. He left the room, closing the large door behind him.

Philintine reached for her goblet on the table, accidentally knocking it to the floor, the wine spilling out—red, like blood.

Chapter 7

Early the next morning Anesia road sidesaddle out the main gate, flanked by two knights. Her sister watched from the wall above. One of the knights turned his head and looked back up toward Philintine, who almost revealed a smile.

Late in the day, the three stopped by a stream to let the horses water. Noron dismounted, went around his horse, reached up for Anesia's waist and with her unspoken permission brought her to the ground. He lifted her as easily as a bag of air, let her go as gently as hands release a dove.

Once their horses had watered, Noron led them to tall grass. Sensing she finally had some privacy with Noron, a knight she had always trusted, she asked him softly, "Where is my father?"

He smiled. "No one knows, probably not even your father. I have gone out with him dozens of times. We seek out the unknown enemy, find squirrels or deer or boar, and bring home a feast. Your father is a hero to the people, and no one tells stories of conflict. So I live here and not someplace else. The greatest fear I have is that a sow will by chance hit my horse and knock me to the ground and run off. I would lose my best horse."

She smiled. "You always told good stories, Noron, even when I was a girl."

He looked at her, as if to say, "You are not still a girl?" But said instead, "You are beginning to be a woman."

"Do you love my sister?"

He was a little surprised by the question, but did not show it much. "I loved your sister. But I think that is all past."

"Did she tell you why she could not love you?"

"Her words were something like, 'I have realized I will one day be queen. And will be my place to marry another king or prince of a great land, be sold like my mother for the betterment of our country.'"

"But if she still loves you…"

"She will marry to protect the State, if she ever becomes queen."

"Even peasants have more say about who they will marry."

"The price royalty pays for having food on the table every day of the year."

"A great price to pay, to marry someone you do not love, could never learn to love. I will not be queen, ever, then, if I have to cut out my heart to wear a crown."

"Many have, and the nations go on."

"But we are more enlightened. Be it only a feeling, I see her with no other but you." She looked at his bearded, handsome face. "I think you are a prince, Noron."

"Great praise from one so royal."

"A cripple."

"Why do you call yourself that? You know your limp is slight."

"Perhaps I feel it more in my heart than my foot."

"Then heal both, and enjoy this ride to your father. If we can find him."

"What will I tell him when I see him? That my drunken sister sent me off?"

"Tell the truth, whatever that may be."

"I love my sister, but she astounds me sometimes."

"She does us all."

"Like when she cut off her long hair. Or when she cut off your relationship so quickly."

He stroked the mane of his horse. "I healed."

"Men heal of the heart faster than women."

"I think you may be right, though not completely."

"You love my father?"

"With all my heart. I came here to be his guard, and he ended up guarding me."

"How do you mean?"

"By giving wine to all foes, we have been without a battle—lest you call boar a battle..." He smiled. "I would surely be dead if anyplace else."

"We have been most fortunate. And to have Darien so close, if needed."

"Twice blessed and ever saved."

"But don't you miss the adventure of battle, as some men do?"

"Once you have ridden or walked across a country, burning the homes of peasants, the adventure is gone. Once you have killed a man, the mystery is gone: his face staring up at you, as if to say, 'I have family back home too, and would rather have been there than here, though I will never be again because of you. You are the same as me, only on this day your sword was quicker. May not be so, next time you meet battle.'"

Anesia said, "I will never ask you so silly a question again."

"Was worth the asking. No, I do not tire of boar hunts. Better boar blood than men's, or mine." Noron noticed a peasant who had come out of the trees along the path they were heading down. He was talking to Toohan, the knight Noron had chosen to come with them.

"I wonder what that is about?" Anesia looked at the men. "Seems serious, whatever the topic."

The peasant glanced at Anesia and Noron separately as he passed them, looked to the ground, then continued along the path.

Toohan came to them. "Unfortunate news. Tor has been gravely injured. Was but earlier this day. The peasant heard a rumor that someone saw them riding as fast as they dare, Tor held up by a knight behind him on his horse, his leg bandaged and full of blood. The peasant who saw them could scarcely tell Tor from the dead."

Anesia almost fainted. Noron held her arm as she went to the ground. "My father…"

Noron said, "He's not dead. You know how tough he is."

Toohan joined them on the ground. They were quiet, Anesia in shock, and the others with feelings and thoughts pounding in.

"Probably from a boar attacking him," Toohan said.

"I pray my father is alive." She briefly held a hand to her face. "May explain the dream I had last night. I dreamt of the sun going out and clouds covering our world. Timeless shook, and fire came out of the ground. The people, in darkness, ran about wildly. I feared the dream was for me, though it may have been a premonition for us all."

Toohan looked at Noron, as if to say, Is Anesia in great danger?

Noron looked away, up to the trees on the far side of the clearing, then said to Toohan quietly, "If Philintine soon be queen, I don't trust her to be kind to Anesia." He looked her way, her eyes closed in some prayer. He clasped his hands together and said a short prayer for Tor and for guidance.

"Father is not dead," Anesia whispered fiercely. "I know it. But I do not know what my sister will do with her newfound power. I fear she may marry me off to some distant kingdom. Or worse."

"Matti will slow her ascent to power," said Noron. "We must wait, or hide. We have a friend not far from here, Caap—"

"The wise old man—" said Toohan.

"He can hide us until we learn of Tor's true fate." To Toohan he said, "You ride hard on the old road north, not passing near the castle, and be to Darien in two days. She and I to Caap's, and wait until you bring Darien and his knights, in case they are needed."

Anesia asked, "Why not all of us to Darien?"

"Every peasant would see you," said Noron. "And rumors would lead Philintine to you quickly, if she wanted you."

"With the second road the only other road north, it is a good plan," said Toohan.

Noron looked at the trees where the peasant disappeared. "If she and I are careful getting to Caap's and no one sees us—would help if the peasant who gave us the news told no one where he saw us."

Toohan said, "Rumors fly faster than birds when news of the royal family is about."

To Anesia, Noron said, "We will have to ride as fast as you can before the trees darken the way to Caap's."

Toohan extended his fist. "Then we do this?"

Noron placed his hand over Toohan's. "Is done."

Anesia added, "With our prayers to Heaven."

Chapter 8

Caap was an old man who lived alone. He kept a few animals, and each spring and fall he asked that boys on neighboring farms help him plant and harvest his fields, which grew smaller and smaller each year. Not because the land was shrinking, but because he was less able to work.

But he somehow managed to keep going. All the farmers had seen him work when he was younger; their sons heard stories of Caap's generosity, helping their fathers or even their grandfathers on lands across the kingdom. It is said that Caap would work from before sunrise to after sunset, from late winter to autumn, on anybody's land that needed work. All the stories told about him were noble and worth telling, even if they had been exaggerated over the years in the retelling.

Caap had grown too poor to buy candles to use at night, so at sundown he was preparing for bed. His house contained a small living room with old furniture, reminders of his famous carpentry skills. Each winter, after the crops were in, he used to make furniture, wooden tools, toys for children, and occasionally an art piece that he freely gave away. Some of the toys had been handed down for two generations. His art adorned the walls and mantels of several of his neighbors' houses. Nowadays, after a few minutes of whittling, his hands were in such pain it was like cutting skin, not wood.

His small bedroom was divided off by a blanket hanging from the doorsill, a blanket his wife had quilted before she died attempting to give birth to their second child, which was stillborn. Their first died the following winter from a fever. Caap never forgave himself for allowing the house to get too cold, or so he thought he had in that way caused the girl's death, though several children in nearby families died the same month from fevers.

He had remained alone all the years, except for an occasional visitor, like the one who knocked on his front door.

"Caap!" Noron called from outside the door. "Caap!" he called again, gently opening the door, which never had a lock on it. "Caap, it's me."

"Noron? Has my friend come to see me?"

"I have a lady visitor. A princess."

"I'm not decent! Wait a minute!" Caap went behind the blanket. "Come in! Come in! Let me get my shirt back on."

The visitors entered. With the door open, there was just enough sunlight to see the little fireplace, two chairs, an old chest and other simple yet finely carved pieces of furniture, and decorations on the mantel and walls. It was a royal house for a poor man.

"Take a chair! Take two chairs! I'll start a fire in a minute."

"I'm not cold," Noron said.

"Nor am I," said Anesia.

"No, to see by. I have no candles." Caap appeared from around the blanket. "Noron." The old man hugged him. "I knew the voice. I could never forget the voice." And the old man looked at the lady. "And your voice I have heard somewhere before. It has also been awhile."

"I'm Anesia."

"*The* Anesia?"

"*The* Anesia," Noron repeated.

"Good Lord. Anesia. Please have a seat if you can see one. Let me start the fire."

Noron said, "Can we stay here a few days, Caap?"

"You are always welcome. Both of you."

"I'll tend to the horses."

As Noron bedded down the horses and hid them as best he could, Caap started a fire. Anesia sat in one of the chairs.

"I would never have thought I would see you in my humble home."

"And I would never have thought my sister would…would send

me off to find Father."

"Where is your father, my girl?"

"He was off hunting, but we heard he has been gravely injured and may be back at the castle by now."

"Don't you want to be by him?"

"Father made Philintine temporary queen before he left and her first act was to send Darien home, and her second was to send me on a horse to find Father. I fear what her next act will be, should she continue as queen."

"Oh dear. So she is already taken by her powers."

"I'm afraid so."

"And what does Matti have to say?"

"She is beyond his power, I guess. Though I hope not totally."

"And the court?"

"They can say little or nothing." She was almost in tears.

Caap sat down, reaching out and touching her arm. "There now, my girl. Your sister is not the violent sort. She has her odd moods, has had for years, but she will not harm you. You know that."

"You have not seen her lately. She has some revenge in her I know not how to describe."

"You will be well here, that I promise. I will gather an army of peasants myself and defend you, if we must."

Anesia smiled. "I thank you for your bravery, but I hardly think your friends would be able to defend against the knights."

"With Noron leading us, no one can defeat us, even if we have but clubs, knives and pitchforks." He took a rod of iron and arranged the sticks on the fire.

They were quiet for a few minutes. Small flames were shooting up as Noron entered.

"I have told Caap our story," said Anesia.

"My home is yours, my children. Anesia can have my humble bed and Noron and I can sleep on the ground in here. We will be warm enough. And I have some food."

Noron said, "We need to be wary of neighbors, she and I staying inside and you tending the horses until news of Tor's fate is known."

"Or Darien rescues us," added Anesia.

"Darien?" Caap was surprised. "You must be truly concerned about your sister if you want Darien to help you."

Noron said, "Another knight, who was with us, is traveling along the old road and can reach Darien in two days."

Caap said, "So we have a few days to wait out. I seldom get visitors here. I'm not the helper I used to be. Now, on this night, two visit me, one of royal blood, and an old friend—Darien perhaps to follow. Quite a night this is. In the next days I'll keep my ear to neighbors' gossip. I'm sure news will spread fast, whatever it is."

Chapter 9

King Tor did return alive, but had lost much blood. One of the
knights had traveled ahead of the group to prepare the doctors and
the surgeon for the coming king.

With no opposing army to be found, on the second day the threat
had been dismissed as rumor, so the fun began. The injury
occurred on Tor's third morning from the castle. The knights
discovered an encampment of boar, and King Tor, not to be
outdone by his younger compatriots, dismounted to flush them
out. Being a bit heavy with drink, he charged through the thick
bushes and trees, sword flailing, more a danger to himself than to a
boar. With several wild animals running about, and unseen men
shouting maneuvers, he was shocked to find a boar horn
protruding through his left calf. He was almost instantly on the
ground, his head hitting a tree trunk along the way. The boar, not
bothering to remove its horn by backing up first, dislodged a huge
chunk of the leg and disappeared into bushes.

Tor screamed in agonizing pain. Once his men found him, the
ones who knew a little about medicine prescribed a bandage to
stop the bleeding, but not much else. So in a ride that lasted into
the night, Tor arrived, half dead from loss of blood and shock.

Once in his room, the medical community quickly rushed to his aid
with more bandages, removing most of the dirt still in the wound.
The bleeding eventually stopped, but the wound looked horrific
each time they changed bandages and added their best potions. In
addition, they had attached worms to his body to suck out bad
spirits. The negative effects of this further loss of blood were not
recorded in their medical books nor spoken of in conventional
wisdom.

By the following evening, Tor's leg was turning shades of blue and green, which all but Tor believed would be fatal without amputation. The surgeon wanted to take off the leg immediately, but could not remove it without the king's permission. Tor, in his delirium, only willing to drink wine to help kill the pain, denied the right to do so. He told the surgeon he had been through worse injuries than this; life would be a bore if sitting on a horse watching his men chase boar. Matti agreed with the surgeon, but was unable to convince Tor.

By the next morning Tor had fallen into a coma. With no nourishment but wine, his body had been given little energy to fight the growing contamination. Tor could not be made to swallow; no food could be gotten in him.

At noon, the surgeon, Matti and the doctors met with Philintine in a closed chamber and pleaded that she overrule her father's hold on his green leg.

"It is my opinion," said the surgeon, "and that of the other doctors, that the malady will soon spread from the leg to his torso. The only relief, but in death, is to remove it immediately."

She only stared at a wall.

"Execute me if you wish for my pleading. I would gladly give my life for his."

She said nothing.

"He is no longer able to decide for himself; only you, my girl, can save him."

"I am not a girl. I am *queen*."

The surgeon looked at Matti, who looked away.

The surgeon moved to the company of the doctors and was quiet.

In a few moments Matti moved to her and said softly, "We love you. You may not believe that, have perhaps never believed that, but we do. And we love your father."

She looked at him angrily.

He continued by pointing out that she now had more than temporary power, and could legally as well as medically save him.

Yet she quoted two subtle Points of Law that Matti thought she had long forgotten, so well argued that he was confounded.

Tor would be king to his death. Matti walked to the door. With the surgeon explaining again to Philintine the seriousness of Tor's condition, Matti left the room mumbling "Snake" under his breath.

Matti passed the guards that Philintine had placed at Tor's door. Tor was unconscious, yet Matti touched his face and told him of the missing daughter. He prayed that Tor regain consciousness. He talked to Tor as if he were conscious, begging him to give up a leg to save a daughter, perhaps a kingdom. Even Matti's prayers and trusted guidance could not awaken him.

Chapter 10

Very early the following morning, Philintine was awakened by a knock at her bedchamber door. Irritated that someone would disturb her before her body could awaken naturally, she said, "Come in!"

Matti entered and closed the door.

"I thought you knew better than to enter a woman's bedchamber."

He was not in a good mood. "I have been with your father the whole night. The surgeon says if we are to save your father the leg must be cut off within the hour."

She said nothing.

"Do you understand the seriousness of this?"

She lay back, staring at the ceiling.

"I said I would make you queen. For God's sake, save the man's life!"

She continued to stare.

He sat on her bed, not looking at her.

"You must think me the most unfeeling creature in the world," she said.

It was his turn to stare silently.

"But you do not know how I have suffered. I have given up my sex to be the son Father wanted."

"You could have been yourself well enough."

"I doubt it."

"I do not." He looked at her face. "I have often wondered what I would do as king, what mistakes I would make. But I do know I would never let my own kin die."

She met his eyes briefly, then stared back at the ceiling.

He forcefully said, "Will you give the surgeon permission?"

She said nothing.

He waited, walked to the door, waited again, looked back at her, opened the door, stepped through it, waited again, then slammed it as hard as he could. The noise resounded through the hall like thunder.

Chapter 11

In about an hour, Philintine found herself at the door to her father's bedchamber. She asked the two guards if Matti was inside and one of them said "No."

She entered the room, where she found the surgeon and a nurse by the bed. She told them to leave the room. They did so.

She sat down in the chair by her father where the nurse had been. The nurse had left the towel on his forehead. Philintine removed it, dropping it to the floor. She stared at her father's face, his mouth open, his breaths barely distinguishable.

Suddenly Tor let out a terrific scream, his arms reaching for his leg. The surgeon opened the door, but before he could come close, Philintine screamed at him, "Stay out!"

The surgeon, with the nurse behind him, withdrew again.

"Does it hurt, Father?"

From his lips came a soft, "Yes," as if he said it any firmer, his teeth would break. He fell back to a lying position. "Wine...wine..."

"You've had enough."

His eyes closed. He was quickly sinking back into a coma.

"I want to know one thing before you die. Did you kill my mother?"

He didn't seem to hear her.

"The price of peace between two nations, the price paid by a woman sold to a kingly bed—the peace that put her to her eternal peace?" She moved close to his ear, but spoke in a normal voice, "Did you kill my mother?"

"No..."

"I know you did. Don't lie to me, Father. Tell me the truth and I'll have them cut off your leg and save your life. Your life depends on the truth, Father."

"No..."

"Your life."

His eyes opened. Softly, "Where's Anesia?"

Angrily, she said, "Who cares about Anesia?"

"Someone...said...she..."

"She's here. Safe. In her room."

"Let me...see her."

"She is afraid you will kill her. You're drunk. You killed her mother. You may kill her."

"No..."

Philintine sat in the nurse's chair. "You will see Anesia when you tell me the truth."

"Who are you? I know you."

She decided to play a game with him. "I am your wife, Terese, with the blond hair."

His head turned slightly toward her; his eyes disbelieved, but his brain was delirious with pain and did little to disagree. "Terese?"

"I hate you. You insisted that I give you a boy. I have never loved you."

"I loved you. As best I could for a woman seen only twice before the arrangement..."

"I have given you another girl."

"A what?"

"A girl." She rose and went close to him. "Remember the night I had your second daughter. Your second disappointment. A girl..."

"Girl..."

"She will have breasts and look like you, a little. But not the beard. She will not carry a sword and be the man you want. In fact, she will become a cripple. A disappointment—again."

"No…" As his head rolled back, he seemed exhausted from the effort it took to carry on a conversation.

"You don't hear the little girl, your oldest daughter, coming down the hall. She heard yelling. You said you didn't want the baby in this room. Not a girl baby. The nurse takes Anesia from me for the first and last time. The door is closed. You yell at me again, in your stupor. The little girl wants to knock on the door, defend me, as best she can for a girl of four. You yell at me again. She is afraid to open the door—you might yell at her. I scream back at you. 'I hate you!' You tell me to be—"

"Quiet."

"I will not be quiet!"

"You will wake the chambers!"

"But your yelling will not?"

"Be quiet!"

"I hate you."

"No…" He was trying to come back to the present.

"I will never give you a boy. I will give girl after girl until you have a room full of them!"

"Who are you?" He leaned up on one arm, toward her.

"I am Terese."

"I know you… God, I'm losing my mind."

"Only your wife…"

"Quiet!" He held a hand up, as if it could deflect the sounds.

She leaned over on the bed so he could better see her face. "Can you not see your own—?"

He suddenly grabbed her by the throat with one quick hand and forced her to lie flat on the bed, her legs dangling off. "Quiet."

Her hands could not break his grip, which seemed to get stronger as she struggled. For the first time in her life her father was using brute force on her.

"Quiet."

She could not breathe. She did not know what her father might do.

"You will be…" His glazed eyes suggested he was reliving the night long ago. "…quiet."

She could not breathe. Was he going to kill her, too?

"Quiet…"

She decided to play dead. Her hands fell, she closed her eyes and lay perfectly still.

He squeezed harder.

She was running out of air. She was dying! By her own father's hand! For the first time in her life she prayed, mentally screaming to Heaven to make him free her.

He relaxed his grip on her neck—she broke away from his hand and fell down to the floor, hitting the chair's leg, gasping for breath. She breathed several times, deeply. What a good feeling, to breathe! She felt the soreness in her neck where his fingers had been. She glanced up—he was not moving. He had fallen face down into a pillow.

She marveled at her own stupidity. Her hate had almost gotten her killed by the same man, in the same drunken stupor. She briefly laughed at her stupidity, relieving some tension. Then she cried. She had not cried so hard since she was that little girl of four. It was true. He had killed her mother. That faint, last struggle and that final silence she heard outside the door were the last moments of her mother's life.

He was making noises, words muffled by the pillow. "You are so weak…like a…bird…"

In a few moments, she rose to her knees, observed him objectively: the nightgown, the now exposed bandages on the green leg, the hair on his head in wild array like a madman's. This is the man she wanted love from? How could she have ever been such a fool?

She rose to her feet. "You killed her. You choked her that night, as I stood outside the door."

"Weak…"

"I know it now."

"No!" he screamed. Suddenly he rolled over in bed, then looked to the other side of the room.

She stepped toward the door, but saw he was not looking near her.

He was staring off into space, his eyes in terror, as if he was meeting his eternal soul. "Terese..."

The impression was so real on his face and in her consciousness that she glanced to the other side of the room where he was looking.

He whispered, "So weak...so strong..."

She had never seen him so vulnerable. For an instant she felt compassion for him—but only for an instant. She stopped the feeling's progress through her body as rapidly as she could.

He was weeping.

Father, crying? This I have never seen. Are you men as weak inside as we are? We women are weak inside and out. Could it be that, in the end, when the killing is done, you are as weak as we are?

His hand was reaching into the space beyond him. Only the rest of his body kept it from going farther.

Something had happened to her in that instant of compassion. She could no longer see him as a murderer, only as a man who had been trained to kill on the battlefield, who had been trained to drink heartily with his fellows, who had been trained to glorify men and to limit the importance of women—who unfortunately had allowed all three beliefs to fall on his wife in one bloody night.

His hand fell and his eyes closed.

He seemed calmer now. She would not torment him anymore. She went closer, to the other side of the bed. Assuring herself that he could not grab her again, she sat on the bed. "Father, are you seeing her?"

His head nodded yes, slightly.

"Is she with you?" That was all she could think to ask.

"Soon..."

"Does...does she hate you?"

He was quiet.

"Tell me..."

He looked at where he thought Philintine's voice had come from. "No." He looked at the vision for a moment, as if to confirm his word. His eyes closed and he rested.

Her eyes were drawn to the dawn's light coming in through the small window. She was not usually drawn to light, but she was at that moment. She looked back at her father. "Die peaceful, Father. Though Heaven may not believe me, I admire you. I have not totally forgotten your good works. If you die, they will remain in the memories of our people...and me. May I be as fortunate, as queen." The dominating presence in the room was silence.

She rose, still looking at him. She wiped away any lingering tears from her face, straightened her dress, and walked to the door. Opening it, the surgeon looked up. "Cut off his leg immediately." She walked down the hall.

"It may be too late," he called.

"Do it!" she ordered.

As she turned a corner she met Matti sitting on the stairs. He had been crying.

"The screams... Is he dead?"

From a lower step, she looked back at him, almost eye to eye. "He confessed." She continued her descent.

Chapter 12

Caap's house, though made many years before by his great carpentry skill and helpful neighbors, was not as stable as it once was, and even less stable after the terrifying scream that awakened the two men lying in the front room. They both thought Anesia had been attacked in the night. They went rushing into her room only to find her sitting up on the bed, sobbing like a child, uncontrollably. Coming closer, they knelt down by her to comfort her.

After several moments she said, "Father is dead. I know it. Father is dead."

That morning, the visitors prepared to leave the country. Since only three days and four nights had passed since they parted with Toohan, Darien could not reach them in time. If Philintine had found out from peasants where they were, her knights could reach them that day. All they could do was hope that Philintine would concentrate on searching peasant houses or assume they had gone north or south on the main road and would not be using the second road north, which was in such poor condition that it was little used. Their plan was to cut across open country, avoid houses, reach the second road and head northward. In the meantime, Caap would spread rumors that someone had seen the couple heading south on the main road.

Chapter 13

That evening, Philintine was sitting alone in the throne room. There was no wine by her side, as before. In her mind, she was visiting, one by one, various rooms in her soul, and finding all of them empty.

She was quietly thinking, not about the State, or her position in it, but about a dead father. And Anesia and Noron—where were they? She had, that afternoon, confirmed the arrangements for her father's burial in two days and had sent knights in all directions in order to find Anesia. But no news would probably come back until tomorrow. She had to find her sister if they were to attend the funeral. Matti had retired to the study and left instructions with a maid that he was not to be disturbed, not even for food. So Philintine instructed the maid to leave plates of food outside the door every few hours. She wondered what Darien might be thinking about her, not that he would care whether she was alive or dead. In fact, probably very few people in the world cared if she was alive or dead. Maybe Anesia cared. Maybe Noron. She had never felt so alone in her life.

She was queen, or would be soon. Oddly enough, being queen mattered very little now. It was, after all, only a title—held by countless people in countless lifetimes, all either dead or holding it now, probably for only a brief time before other nations or their own courts took it away. And the only things all the kings and queens left behind after they were gone were people, and memories of good deeds in the minds of their people or written down in books like Matti's. She had neither people nor good deeds.

Her first three acts as queen had been to rudely dismiss their closest ally, send off her sister to possible injury, and kill her father by neglect of an obviously serious wound. How many more stubborn and foolish acts could she commit before the people of her country would either banish her or imprison her? They would take Anesia as queen and let her marry Darien, absorbing themselves into a larger country, then protected by wine and an army. Philintine could not, she told herself, be more foolish than she had been. For all her mental prowess, she had absolutely no wisdom. No "heart," as Darien or Matti might call it. She was in the unique position of having gained all the world and lost it at the same time.

A single candle lit the room. Could she be such a candle to her country? She might be small, but the whole room was dimly lit by it. Could she light her country? She knew what her father would say. He used to tell her he was but one light, one small candle, but when joined by the lights of his close advisors and loved ones, was bright enough to warm and illuminate his whole kingdom. Philintine suddenly felt that if she were to attempt to regain the other lights in her life, she might be able to fully light the room. It was not too late. The candle had not yet gone out.

She wondered if one of the few bits of wisdom that she had ever garnered was coming to her now: She had caused this aloneness to happen to her, and if she had caused it to happen, she could cause something else to happen, replace it with something much better.

No, she could not bring her father back to life, but she could bring children into the world. Funny, she had never given any thought to having a child. But if she and Noron did, the child must be called Tory, or Tor, or something like that. And if a girl, Tornia—or some name Noron could choose.

Remarkably, perhaps even the Spirit of a dead father could be happy over his daughter's new-found belief in love and its power. Her sex, which she had despised, could be her salvation. Through giving birth to a baby, she might give some recompense to God, or whatever was in control, for a dead father. Her breasts, which she once said she wished she could cut off, would nurse the infant. Her arms, which she wanted to make stronger, would be strong enough to hold a baby up to its father.

A great deal of good must be done, and done quickly.

Chapter 14

Philintine, not being a woman of convention, donned riding clothes and a black scarf rather than a black dress of mourning on the morning after her father passed into a world where wine is more imagination than substance. Armed with the news that Noron and Anesia were heading north on the second-best road, she galloped out of the castle with two knights behind her. When they entered the old road, one of the knights, who was especially gifted at tracking, inspected the way north. "Two horses! Recently!" he yelled. And they were off.

The old road was treacherous. Wagon tracks over the years had made deep ruts, growing worse each year during the rainy season because of wagons that had to pass over the road to reach a few small farms it still supplied. Parts of the road were through steep hills, so narrow in places that barely a wagon could pass.

But Philintine galloped hard. She slowed only when she had to, when her horse might be in danger of tripping in ruts and breaking a leg. A horse with a broken leg would be useless; it was better to not blame the horse for the conditions, but to go slower at times. And too, her gray stallion was her favorite mount.

As she galloped, she thought more about her father. Yes, he had killed her mother, but she was the last person in their whole country to die from royal violence. Since that day, Tor had never fought man or woman. He proved by his actions that he was truly sorry. When armies threatened, he took in the warring ones and made them friends, gave land to neighbor countries when they needed it, sent as many of his people that he could to help harvest the crops of neighboring countries when their crops were more than bountiful. No other country had ever done that before. Perhaps neighbor kings thought him a fool, to give grapes and land so easily, to send his people as laborers. But they still took the wine and the help. And over the years, Tor had received land and shared bounty from neighbors in about the same proportion as he had given. Most kings respected him; those who didn't, at least tolerated him. As queen, if she had the courage, or the sense of humor, to follow his lead, perhaps she could create a second generation of wine giving and peace.

Before noon, she saw Anesia and Noron ahead; Anesia was sidesaddle, not cross-legged like she rode. Norton's free hand was in hers, helping her ride steady. Philintine stopped, as did her knights; she told them to remain there—she would ride ahead alone. They waited a few horse lengths, then disobeyed her command, fearing for her safely in case Noron felt threatened. As Philintine followed at the pace of the couple, her escorts followed her. She looked again at Noron's hand touching Anesia's.

Her sister, the meek cripple, not as attractive, not as powerful, had brought home the love of two men—the two men Philintine had cared most for, who behind her back would call her Snake. All the power of the kingdom, all sternness, all the Points of Law could not do what her sister had done by doing little more than smiling, clapping, and waving people on. Anesia had conquered her world. And the man Philintine loved most was holding her hand as gently as he had once held hers. There, ahead, were the two people who loved her most—amazing that anyone still did.

It was Anesia who first noticed the travelers behind them. She let out a small scream of fear.

Noron looked at her, then looked back. He said to Anesia, "Ride on ahead, as fast as you can."

"I may never see you again."

"Go." When she hesitated, he said "Go," more strongly. And she was off, as fast as she dare.

He whirled his horse and drew his sword. He rode toward Philintine.

Philintine's horse stopped, perhaps of its own volition. It was her turn to be afraid. She had never seen an armed man coming toward her. Not realizing that Noron was looking behind her at her escorts, who had drawn their swords after he drew his, she was frozen in fright. She could not move. When he came close, she could see he was not looking at her. She understood. She turned her body and screamed at her knights, "He won't kill me, you idiots! He's my husband!"

All three men stopped their horses. When she looked back at Noron, he was looking into her eyes.

He looked to the knights, who were ready to tear him limb from limb should he try anything. Noron called them by name, then smiled. He fiercely threw his sword into the trees and bushes.

Philintine turned to her escort. "He is my husband, or will be. He will not hurt me. Sheathe your swords." They did so. "Now go back a ways and let us have privacy." They turned and went back, out of hearing distance.

When she turned to look again at Noron, his horse was beside hers. "When I saw your hand in Anesia's, I saw not only what I was missing, but I saw how my father and mother, young, could have been. Like a window of Heaven opened above this shallow road, I passed through it in mind and saw Father and Mother reunited— not in hate as I imagined, but love. My mother has forgiven him. I have also."

He looked at her golden hair, so fresh, so clean, blowing slightly in the breeze. "Tor is dead?"

"He has passed where my mother is. Not dead. Together, living in some other world. I feel it so."

"Will be a great change for our country. For me."

"You are welcome here as long as you want to stay." She looked down the road. "I am tired of fighting—the world, and myself. I have killed a man."

He looked at her, as if he had asked, "Who?"

"My father. By neglect of an obviously serious wound. I could have saved him, but instead wanted a selfish confession for something that happened so long ago, and so paid for by him, that it was not worth my years of anger and hate—if anything is."

"I am sorry to hear of his passing."

"Do not be. They are happier now together than they ever were. But I am judged, a fool—less than a court jester. A fool in the truest sense. And I do not have even wine to blame for it. I have killed a man, so that makes me less than a drunken man."

"No, it makes you another member of the sad lot of humanity."

"I hurt so for him, but I cannot bring him back."

"You are now believing in feelings, and not reason?"

"Both." She looked at him briefly, then into the trees. "I have not been on this road for a long time, not since you were banished from my heart. Can you be open to it again? I would not blame you if you could not."

"Are you proposing marriage?"

Philintine smiled. "I have been like a man so long, I guess I take liberties."

"Then let me, like a woman, consider. You come here a new person, and with news of your father. I need time to think, and learn your new heart."

"I have time, and peace, for the first time since I was a little girl. It is my peace I most want to share with you, and my country, which I love. And father loved, in his way. When you first came here, the strong, handsome knight, ready to defend Father, I think I fell in love with you on sight. Within a year, you were teaching me to ride."

"My bravest and best student, who today rides the gray stallion."

"Then I left you emotionally."

"You left all of us."

"Was about the time I assumed the role of queen in my mind. I felt

I should not become attached to you if I were to be married to some other prince or king for my country's sake. And too, it frightened me to think of assuming the care for thousands of people."

"As Caap would say, 'They are not in your care alone, but in God's.'"

"But will I decide rightly for them?"

"God will give you the guidance you need."

"Can I protect them in times of threats?"

"Grapevines have stopped all past armies, and Matti's powers of persuasion. Why should that change? And before Matti passes on to be with your father and mother, he can probably teach you his ways."

"If I listen."

"I listen to Caap, who carved a brace for Anesia; she walks with no limp now."

"Caap, the Matti of the peasants."

"Matti, the Caap of the royal family."

"We are twice blessed."

"Blessed in taking faith for fear."

"Be it so. If I can forgive Father, I can forgive myself for being the fool."

"Such a short-time fool, with much time left to make amends."

"I will. I promise. And I promise to look after my sister." She looked back down the road. "So let's go stop her from killing herself." She kicked and her horse shot off like a hawk on a chase.

Noron called to her escort, "Our country has found peace, my brothers! Let's go find Anesia!" He turned his horse on the narrow road and charged after her.

The two knights looked at each other, smiled at the thought of a friendly chase, and kicked their horses.

Noron could not gain on Philintine's horse even though it had been galloping for hours. In fact, her stallion was lengthening the lead. Less than a mile farther on, just over a steep hill with deep wagon ruts from a recent rain, Philintine's horse almost tripped; she held on for life and slowed down. Nearby was Anesia's horse, riderless, limping and obviously hurting.

Not seeing her sister anywhere, Philintine was afraid she had been thrown off and might lay injured beside the road. She looked around near the horse, calling "Anesia! Anesia!" Then she turned and went back quickly.

Noron almost ran into her at the hill. The knights, right behind him, passed her, each to one side, with inches to spare. The men were confused until they too saw the riderless horse. Philintine began calling, "Anesia, forgive me! Anesia!" Then the men started calling her name.

Philintine, seeing no sign, turned her horse and headed again toward Anesia's.

Anesia, hearing Noron's voice, realized that some truce had been struck between the parties. She called out from the trees where she had limped in fear for her life. "I'm here! I'm here!"

Philintine was the first to the place, dismounted, and rushed to her sister. Her concern was obvious in her face.

"I hurt my other ankle. Double cripple." Anesia started to cry, from the pain and the humiliation, and the happiness at being saved.

Philintine looked at the hurt ankle. She could tell it was not serious. "You didn't help the horse, either. Is this your revenge on horses for that throw when you were eight?" She smiled.

Anesia smiled through her pain and tears.

"You men! Help her to my horse. She has two bad legs, now. Leave the wounded horse to the peasants, but not her saddle."

Chapter 15

The following morning the sun rose to greet the castle courtyard as the people moved slowly about their affairs. Tor would be buried that afternoon, with Matti giving the eulogy. Everyone in the castle and most of the people in outlying areas would be attending. Tor had been their peace king, the one who had, in a stupor, kept their blood flowing in their bodies long enough to see their sons and daughters marry and create their own sons and daughters. Tor had died in agony, so rumor had it, but he was killed fighting a boar as wild and senseless as he. They loved him, even more now that he was gone. They were in mourning even at work.

Strangely enough, his burial might be unattended by his two daughters, one of whom was at that moment tracking down the other, perhaps to kill her or bring her back to a prison cell. Some talk passed among the peasants that Matti might lead a hoped-for proceeding against Philintine if she killed or imprisoned her sister, denying Philintine the ordination and allowing Darien to rule in absence of a good leader. But peasant talk was not serious talk. They would endure as they always had, generations living a modest existence, enduring by hope and faith more than royal justice.

The relative quiet of the town gave way to shouting from a turret where guards were saying they could not believe their eyes, and using words like "miracle." Boys rushed to the gate to see down the road, where Anesia and Philintine were on Philintine's gray stallion, Noron riding behind, followed by the escort. Around them was a small crowd of peasant farmers with a few wives and children, walking, cheering, clapping, and shouting words like, "Two queens! Peace forever!" "Long live the queens of love!" "Praise be the two sisters!"

The word spread like fire. Merchants and their wives stopped their work. By the time the travelers reached the gate, most of the citizens had come out to see them, cheering, applauding, singing, and throwing flowers and grass and hay. All the guards atop the walls had left their posts and were above them, cheering and talking.

By the time the riders entered the town, the noise had disturbed Matti from his books. Out a window in the study, he observed Noron dismounting, reaching up for Anesia, and then Philintine. The sisters wore crowns of flowers on their heads. Tears came to Matti's eyes. The kingdom had somehow been restored; two sisters were now love.

As hundreds cheered, with hats thrown in the air, boys and men on horses streamed from the castle, spreading the news to every house and barn or traveler in the kingdom. It was, by far, the quickest truth or rumor ever spread across the land.

Chapter 16

Just after dawn the next morning, Darien returned to the town, but not in his usual attire. He and a few of his best knights entered through the east gate, dressed as peasants, their weapons hidden in their clothing, in a bundle of hay one of them carried over his shoulder, and under hay in a small wagon two of them pulled.

They were surprised at what they saw. Not only were the walls totally unguarded, inside were bodies everywhere: leaning against buildings, lying in walkways, hung over chairs, on the ground as if they had fallen there. All were sleeping gently, some snoring. A single musician, seated by a fountain, his fellow musicians lying about him, played a song on his guitar and sang—not in his usual excellence, for his fingers and tongue were as light-headed as the rest of him.

"Way oh, the town does roll
and as we go—we go—
to dreams of paradise
and all we know—we know.
Way—" He stopped upon seeing the visitors, but with
his vision not able to distinguish faces in the dawn's light,
he sang on as if he had not been disturbed.

Darien thought, *Must be some kind of wake for Tor, who is dead for sure.* He gave signals to his men, and they spread out according to their plan to find Anesia. In a few minutes, Darien and two of his men, after not finding her in her quarters, entered the throne room. He saw a woman facing the throne, in her royal robe, a crown atop her head. He could see no one else about. The three of them closed the two large doors behind them and Darien alone came near the robed figure. "I have come to ask you to give me your sister."

There was no answer.

"From the look of your kingdom, your father is dead."

"Yes. A boar. He was buried yesterday and my people celebrate my rise to power."

"Does grieve me greatly to hear of his passing. I loved him as my own father."

"A drunk."

"No. A noble man who kept peace in his own way for a generation. Were I so brave or wise."

"This land is in great danger without a marriage between you and me."

"I pray you not ask me to unite our lands in this way, but give me Anesia. I promise that by my love and bond to her there will forever be a defense of your land by us. I pray her love will be enough of an alliance to satisfy you, perhaps softening you in time, to see that our kingdoms round about need no greater alliance."

"My knight, Toohan, reached you?"

"Yes, as we were making plans to leave the next morning."

She paused. "Then you knew beforehand, and have spies in my land."

"Was Tor's, then. He would not care. One of my first acts as king was to ask for volunteers to come and live here to watch over

Anesia. I have a small army in the woods, insisted on by my court to ensure my safety, come in wagons, then a running march through the woods to save her. Rumor has it that you brought her back in some temporary truce. Where is she?"

"She is beside Father."

"You mean at the grave?"

"She is beside Father."

"You have not had her killed?"

There was no answer.

"Answer me. Is she dead?" He clutched his dagger's hilt.

There was no answer.

He looked back at his knights, who looked down or away. He turned again to the robed figure. "Tell me direct that you have not killed her."

She said nothing.

Darien drew his hidden dagger. "I could kill you. A snake to die for the killing of a dove, who was loved by all. Any sister who would end the life of a sister—"

"A cripple."

"A dove, who in her presence all animals took refuge, and at night the stars set forth their most radiant shine to copy her. In the name of mercy, God, all that is good among our people, tell me she is not dead."

"She has the peace she deserves."

"You *did* have her killed?"

Silence.

His voice filled with emotion. "Why?" Then growing softer, "So gentle a spirit, harmless to you except in jealousy. You Snake. You never loved anybody. You have no right to kill anybody. Especially not one so lovely."

"A cripple."

He pressed the dagger point into her side.

She closed her eyes.

Darien said, "I could this day pronounce myself king of both lands. Killing of the hateful sister who laid low so sweet a one would be a welcomed relief to your father's people. All called her sister, even peasants who but saw her face once, saw her love, and loved her. Loved by all life near her, till you killed her."

One of the knights stepped forward and spoke, "The peasants may not easily take to our rule gained from ugly murder, even though with some justice."

Darien continued as if the knight had not spoken. "No one would know. It would be the greatest day in the life of this kingdom. You have them drunk now, as drunk as your father was."

The knight said, "They would know it was you who did this."

"Where there's blood for blood—does not this evil treachery of jealous sister chasing after another call for revenge? I could kill you!"

"Could mean war," pleaded the knight. "Without anyone to guide them, the peasants might take any leader and march on us."

Darien still seemed to ignore the knight. "To take one life so vile as yours...and cause a thousand good ones to fall. To see on field, bloody grain—corpses, the wounded being led off on either side, as my father. Too many to bury—the blood you caused... And I. If I can be but the man your father was, who harmed no one—"

"Only my mother, whom he killed."

"Was in childbirth, they say. At worst, an accident. Mine would not be." He dropped the dagger. The sound of its fall against the wooden floor echoed around the room.

The woman's eyes opened again.

"I loved your father, and will commit no great crime to his daughter, though she be but half a human. For him, I leave us living on both sides. And you in your hate-filled contempt of love, be it father's or sister's or mine! Though some may call me weak, I will hold to his silent strength." He closed his eyes, in tears, as his head bowed.

"As do I, my Lord." The lady turned.

The closest knight, seeing an unexpected face, was not sure at first.

"Not weak," she said. "But strong. To not take revenge, leave all to Heaven's justice, is virtue. And love."

The knight, sure now, screamed to his fellow knight, "Anesia!" The knights ran to each other and hugged in joy.

Darien opened his eyes and saw not his hate, but his love.

Anesia spoke softly. "Forgive me. From view above I saw your men enter the yard and came here, thinking you might. I disguised myself in this robe and my sister's voice to test your love. I would rather die than marry a man who would take a life in revenge."

The knight turned to Darien. "Beg pardon, Lord. May we go tell the others and the army?"

"Yes," said Darien. "Tell them this is my bride and soon our queen."

The knights excitedly left the room, yelling for joy.

"There's wine enough for all!" Anesia called after them, smiling.

"I almost killed you."

"Yet you did not." She held his head in her hands. "We are not children in love, and so must act our mature parts." She kissed his face, then rested her head on his shoulder. "Your love kept me from harm. I knew I was safe." Then she admitted, "Well, fairly safe."

"So difficult a test I have never passed."

"I know you well enough to trust you with my life."

"And your sister's." He hugged her. "As I trust you with my kingdom, if I should die soon."

"You will not. Our wine will keep us safe—and Heaven." She felt his strong shoulders, able to help hold up a world of love.

He felt her crown, and moved back from her. "You wear a crown of flowers?"

"Made by my good sister."

"'Good'?"

"Since we both be queens soon, we made crowns of flowers for each other. With patience, a snake can take wings with a dove."

Philintine and Noron entered the room, coming forward hand in hand. Philintine, wearing her crown of flowers, pretended to be upset. "What are the noises we heard from those men? I turn my back and look who appears, in peasant's garb, holding my sister's arm in a room of State!"

Darien said, "I hope it is permitted now."

"Encouraged." Philintine bowed to him at the head, as did Darien to her, and she wrapped an arm around her sister. "Dear one, what is this man doing to you?"

"By pretending to be you, he almost killed me."

Philintine looked at him suspiciously. "Really?" Then brushed it off. "Well, no matter. Is forgiven. I almost did, too."

"And he has proposed to me."

"Proposed what?"

"Marriage."

"What did you tell him?"

"Yes."

"Good." Philintine kissed her face. She moved to Noron and took his hand. "And I with the love of my life, who taught me to ride and will teach me more…"

"And Matti to unite us," said Noron.

Philintine said to them all, "We need to put Matti to work, marrying one, then the other."

"Or all at once," suggested Darien.

Anesia said, "Wonderful idea."

"In whose court?" asked Philintine.

"It matters little," said Darien, "we being now so close."

Noron suggested, "Why not both marriages in the country between our courts?"

"Yes," agreed Anesia, "with Darien's counselor and priests present, at some half-way point between our lands—"

"In a clearing," added Darien. "I passed by one coming here—my great concern now turned to easy care."

Noron said, "With as many peasants as can attend—Caap included."

"It is done," said Philintine. "Joint marriages by Matti in the presence of both courts and all who wish to come."

Anesia said, "With Heaven's blessings—and Father's. And with my new husband's consent, I want to bring Caap to my court as a counselor and friend." To Darien she commented, "You will like him."

Darien smiled.

Noron said, "At last the wise old man will have money for candles and be a light to a nation."

Philintine squeezed Noron's hand. "Let's give Matti the good news."

"Then," said Anesia, "we to Father's grave, with flowers."

"Though his Spirit is most likely out chasing boar someplace," said Noron, smiling.

"I felt him right here," said Anesia to Darien. "When earlier I said, 'She is beside Father,' I felt him beside me. Do you think me strange?"

No one said so.

"Then if he is here," said Philintine, "may he also hear an older daughter's request for forgiveness about a leg not cut soon enough."

Anesia paused. "He hears. And forgives. Forgive him for Mother—and all of you, forget any and all crimes he committed while in drink."

"And let us learn to use wine in moderation, lest we make mistakes," Philintine added, thoughtfully.

Darien said, "Agreed."

Anesia took her sister's other hand. "Then to our future loves."

Anesia and Philintine stepped over the dagger as the couples, hand in hand, left the room. In less than an hour they had told a laughing Matti, visited the gravesite, and were playing in the countryside beyond, as Timeless children often did.

ABOUT THE AUTHOR AND THE PUBLISHER

About the Author

John Schmidt has published almost two dozen works, through his publishing company, Path Publishing, other publishers, and ebook publishers. For more than two decades he has been the editor of Path Publishing, releasing the works of more than twenty authors. In addition, he has earned Master's Degrees in English and in Drama; spent several years teaching college and high school English; penned more than 4,000 poems; developed skills for writing in several genres, from nonfiction books to plays to poems to short stories; and has always encompassed a great love for creative expression and the human experience. He lives in Amarillo, Texas, and is the Membership Coordinator for the Hi-Plains Poetry Society and Inspirational Writers Alive!, Amarillo Chapter.

About Path Publishing

Path Publishing began in 1993 and has published a variety of uplifting books and other projects over the years. The company tends to specialize in Christian nonfiction, poetry, biographies, and self-help. The website, pathpublishing.com, contains the works of numerous writers. In the past, the company has been in these publications: *Christian Writers' Market Guide*, *The Directory of Little Magazines and Small Presses*, and *The Writer*.

Books and Ebooks by John Schmidt

Most of John's works can be ordered using PayPal at
www.pathpublishing.com. Many book descriptions are at
www.pathpublishing.com. On menu bar, click on "Most of the
Books by John Schmidt" or "Personal Page for John."

You can also order paper editions or the audio book by mail. The
cost of the paperback edition of *Timeless Sisters* is $5.99. Postage is
$3.50 for the first item and 75 cents for each additional. With the
shipping, the cost of one book is only $9.48. Texas residents need
to add 8.25 percent sales tax which comes to $10.26. Send bank
check to Path Publishing, 4302 SW 51st Ave. #121, Amarillo,
Texas 79109-6159. For inquiries, e-mail path@pathpublishing.com.
The cost of the Smashwords ebook edition of *Timeless Sisters* is
$2.99 and can be ordered at Smashwords.com or its many apps.
Thank you!

Other paperbacks for adults:

Rock Solid Concrete Poems—Art Poems for the Heart, $7.99.

*Winner's Wisdom—Eight-Week Devotional Using Poetry and Journaling to
Express the Real You*, $8.99.

My Return to the Future, 2350—Our Next Great Civilization Revealed,
$9.99.

Forty Tips for Church Growth—A how-to guide for practical expansion,
$4.99. Also an ebook for the same price at Smashwords.com.

Friends Forever, You and God—A Coloring Book for Adults and Children,
$5.50.

My Visit to the Kingdom of God, $13.99.

Giving to Yourself and Letting Happiness Happen, $6.99.

Our Dream Language, $5.95.

Utopia II—An Investigation into the Kingdom of God, $3.50.

Audio book:

Silly Willy Will, a two-cassette collection of John's poetry, $6.00.

Paperbacks for youths:

The Lion Princess—Journey to an Awakening, $12.95.

Heroes, Angels and Miracles—Eleven Uplifting Stories from Around the World for Youths, $25.00, 360 pages. "Timeless Sisters" is one of the stories in this book.

Children's books:
Purchase all three for only $10.00.

Mr. Turtle's Award, $6.00.

You and God Together, Friends Forever, $6.00.

Two Stories for Children—Betty Blooper Is Super! and Hands Holding Heaven, bilingual, English and Spanish, $6.00.

His Smashwords ebooks:

Timeless Sisters, $2.99.

Forty Tips for Church Growth—A how-to guide for practical expansion, $4.99.

Connect with John Schmidt

By e-mail: path@pathpublishing.com

Check out www.pathpublishing.com for more information about his books. On menu bar, click on "Most of the Books by John Schmidt" or "Personal Page for John."

Amazon.com Author Page:
https://authorcentral.amazon.com/gp/books/book-detail-page?ie=UTF8&bookASIN=1500531316&index=default

Facebook John Schmidt: www.facebook.com/john.schmidt.716195

Facebook Path Publishing: www.facebook.com/pages/Path-Publishing/110081005733297?sk=notes

LinkedIn: www.linkedin.com/in/path-publishing-35097434/

Final words from John: "Many thanks to my readers! Please remember to leave a review for my book at your favorite retailer."

www.ingramcontent.com/pod-product-compliance
Lightning Source LLC
Chambersburg PA
CBHW071628140626
46555CB00021B/1470